E   (Replacement)
Tu Tudor, Tasha
    Pumpkin moonshine.

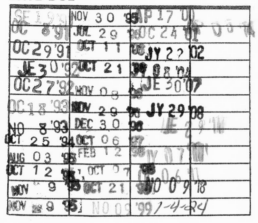

PUMPKIN
MOONSHINE

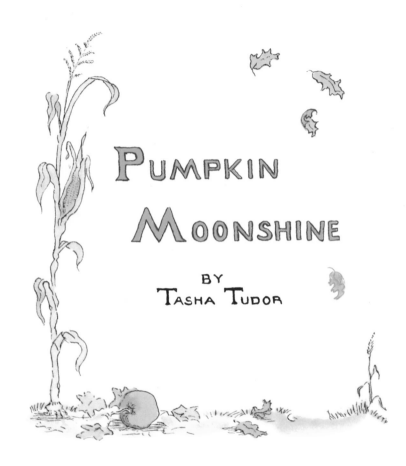

PUMPKIN MOONSHINE

BY
TASHA TUDOR

Random House New York

Library of Congress Cataloging-in-Publication Data:
Tudor, Tasha. Pumpkin moonshine / by Tasha Tudor.   p.   cm. SUMMARY: A little girl visiting her grandparents sets out to find a fine pumpkin for Halloween, and it leads her on a merry chase when it rolls down the hill.   ISBN: 0-394-84588-9   [1. Halloween— Fiction. 2. Pumpkin—Fiction] I. Title.   PZ7.T8228Pu   1989   [E]—dc19   89-3543

Manufactured in the United States of America   1 2 3 4 5 6 7 8 9 0

 UMPKIN

 OONSHINE

A WEE STORY

FOR A VERY SWEET WEE PERSON

SYLVIE ANN WAS VISITING HER GRANDMUMMY IN CONNECTICUT. IT WAS HALLOWE'EN AND SYLVIE WANTED TO MAKE A PUMPKIN MOONSHINE, SO SHE PUT ON HER BONNET AND STARTED OUT FOR THE CORNFIELD TO FIND THE VERY FINEST AND LARGEST PUMPKIN.

HE CORNFIELD WAS ON TOP OF THE HILL, QUITE A WAY FROM THE HOUSE, SO SYLVIE TOOK WIGGY FOR COMPANY.

THE HILL WAS VERY STEEP, IT MADE SYLVIE AND WIGGY PUFF LIKE STEAM ENGINES.

WHEN THEY REACHED THE FIELD, SYLVIE LOOKED AMONG THE SHOCKS OF CORN FOR THE VERY FATTEST PUMPKIN. WAY ACROSS THE FIELD SHE FOUND SUCH A FINE ONE!

T WAS SO VERY BIG
SYLVIE COULDN'T LIFT IT. SO
INSTEAD SHE ROLLED IT ACROSS
THE FIELD, JUST THE WAY YOU
ROLL BIG SNOW BALLS IN
WINTERTIME.

BUT WHEN SYLVIE AND WIGGY AND THE PUMPKIN CAME TO THE EDGE OF THE FIELD WHERE THE GROUND SLOPED DOWN INTO THE BARNYARD BELOW, THE PUMPKIN BEGAN RUNNING AWAY!

It LEAPT OVER STONES AND BUSHES! BUMPITY, BUMP, BUMP! FASTER, FASTER DOWN THE HILL WITH SYLVIE AND WIGGY RUSHING AFTER IT.

T FRIGHTENED THE

GOATS!

T TERRIFIED THE

HENS!

T ENRAGED THE GEESE, AS IT TORE INTO THE BARNYARD AT A TRULY DREADFUL SPEED.

BUT WORST OF ALL
IT BUMPED RIGHT INTO MR.
HEMMELSKAMP WHO WAS
CARRYING A PAIL FULL OF
WHITEWASH!

IT DIDN'T STOP TILL IT HIT THE SIDE OF THE HOUSE —KER THUMPITY, BUMPITY, THUMP!

SYLVIE ANN WAS A VERY POLITE LITTLE GIRL, SO OF COURSE SHE HELPED MR. HEMMELSKAMP TO HIS FEET BEFORE GOING AFTER THE PUMPKIN. SHE APOLOGIZED TO THE GOATS AND POULTRY TOO.

HEN SYLVIE WENT TO
HER GRANDPAWP AND TOLD HIM
WHAT HAPPENED, SO HE CAME
OUT AND CUT THE TOP OFF
THAT RUNAWAY PUMPKIN.

YLVIE SCOOPED ALL THE
SEEDS AND PULP OUT, THEN
GRANDPAWP MADE EYES AND
A NOSE AND A BIG GRINNING
MOUTH WITH HORRID CROOKED
TEETH.

I T WAS EVENING BY
THEN SO THEY PUT A LIGHTED
CANDLE INSIDE THE PUMPKIN
TO MAKE HIM LOOK AS FIERCE
AND HORRID AS ALL TRUE
PUMPKIN MOONSHINES SHOULD.

YLVIE AND GRANDPAWP
PUT THE PUMPKIN MOONSHINE
ON THE FRONT GATE POST,
THEN THEY HID IN THE BUSHES
TO WATCH HOW TERRIFIED
THE PASSERS BY WOULD BE
AT THE SIGHT OF THIS FIERCE
PUMPKIN MOONSHINE. THEY
HAD A WONDERFUL TIME.

YLVIE ANN SAVED THE
PUMPKIN SEEDS. NEXT SPRING
SHE PLANTED THEM. THE VINES
GREW UP AND RAN ALL OVER
THE CORNFIELD, WITH LOTS OF
PUMPKINS ON THEM, JUST
WAITING TO BE MADE INTO
PUMPKIN PIES AND PUMPKIN
MOONSHINES TO PLEASE GOOD
LITTLE GIRLS LIKE SYLVIE ANN.

THE END